SCARY FRIGHT, ARE YOU ALL RIGHT?

Scott Gibala-Broxholm

DIAL BOOKS FOR YOUNG READERS
NEW YORK

Published by Dial Books for Young Readers
A division of Penguin Putnam Inc.
345 Hudson Street
New York, New York 10014

Designed by Kimi Weart
Text set in Bernhard Modern
Printed in Hong Kong

1 3 5 7 9 10 8 6 4 2

Library of Congress Cataloging-in-Publication Data
Gibala-Broxholm, Scott.
p. cm.
Summary: After playing with a new human friend, a monster girl
named Scary Fright begins behaving strangely—choosing a kitten for a pet,
developing a taste for pizza, and drawing rainbows on her wall.
ISBN 0-8037-2588-4 (hc trade)
[1. Monsters—Fiction. 2. Behavior—Fiction.] I. Title.
PZ7.G339095 Sf 2002
[E]—dc21   00-025815

The full-color artwork was prepared using pencil and watercolor washes.

With love to my parents,
who always believed in me and let me believe
—and—
For Charles Addams and his frightfully funny family

A "SCARY" PROBLEM

Scary Fright was a perfect monster. She growled. She howled—and she snarled too. Her favorite game was hide-and-shriek. And she loved to prowl the graveyard late at night.

Scary lived in a creepy old house with her mama, papa, and baby brother, Boo. Sometimes she had monstrous tantrums. Her eyes lit up, her head spun around, and purple smoke came out of her ears.

This always made her parents very proud of their little monster.

Everything was going frightfully well until one Friday the thirteenth. Scary had just stomped home after playing with a new friend.

"Look what I found!" she yowled.

"WHAT is that THING?" snarled Papa.

"It's called a kitten," Scary explained.

"Well, you can have it for dessert," Mama told her. "But only if you eat all your slime."

"No, Mama! I want to keep it for a pet," Scary replied.

Mama's eyes popped out and rolled across the floor. She popped them back in.

"But it's so soft and cuddly and . . . CUTE!" Mama screeched.

"Wouldn't you rather have a bat or a spider for a pet?" asked Papa.

"I WANT a KITTEN!" demanded Scary. She was about to have a monster-sized tantrum.

But just then, the kitten gently rubbed up against her leg. "Meow?" it asked.

"Please, Mama? Please, Papa?" Scary said instead.

"Well . . . " Mama began.

"Oh, THANK YOU!" Scary purred.

Mama and Papa were shocked.

"She's *so* polite!" Papa shuddered.

"And a kitten for a pet?" Mama shivered.

"Good goblins! What's next?"

SUPPERTIME

It was midnight and time for supper. The clock
on the wall screamed twelve times as a rotten
smell drifted from the pot on the stove.

"I made your favorite dish," Papa said to Scary. "Spiderweb soup—with extra slime."

"I want pizza!" Scary told him.

"What's that?" Papa asked.

"It's something humans eat," she said.

Papa's jaw dropped to the floor.

Mama bit her spoon in half.

Baby Boo just smiled and sucked his pointy
thumb.

"I think I know how to make it," Scary told
them.

First she rolled out some mold for the dough.
Then she used slimy moss to make the sauce.
Next she sprinkled on fleas for the cheese. And
for the topping: ten beetles hopping!

When it was done, everyone tried a slice.
"Yummm," Mama said while she munched and
crunched. "It's horribly good."

After supper the whole family went outside.

Mama, Papa, and Baby Boo howled at the moon.

"A-r-r-oooo-oo!"

But Scary sang "Twinkle, Twinkle, Little Star" just as loud as she could.

"That . . . song." Mama trembled. "It's SO sweet and . . . PRETTY!"

"Go to your room!" Papa thundered. "And don't stomp out until you can behave like a monster."

Scary stormed back into the house and
stomped upstairs.

Then she took out her crayons and began to draw on her walls.

All of a sudden she heard pawsteps. Then shadows appeared beside her door.

"*Cre-e-e-ak!*" Slowly the door opened.

"Eee-eee-ahh-ahh!" screamed Mama.

"For goodness' snakes!" growled Papa.

"Isn't it beautiful?" Scary asked.

"But those are butterflies and rainbows!" Papa grunted.

"What about a fire-breathing dragon or a spooky headless ghost?" asked Mama.

"I like butterflies and rainbows better," yowled Scary.

"That's IT!" Papa roared. "We're taking you to see Doctor Ghastly!"

So Grandma Gloom crept over to monster-sit Baby Boo.

Mama, Papa, and Scary climbed on the family broomstick and, with a puff of green smoke, they flew away.

AT DOCTOR GHASTLY'S

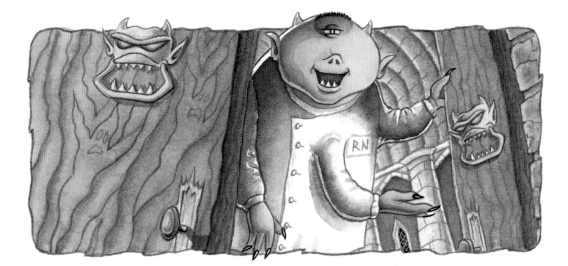

Nurse Eek welcomed them to the office.

Doctor Ghastly looked Scary over from head
to tail. She took her temperature and listened to
both her hearts beat.

"Has Scary played with any human children?" asked the doctor.

"Gadspooks, NO!" Papa snorted.

"Oh yes I did!" said Scary.

"You DID?" Papa groaned.

Mama chewed her claws.

"Mr. and Mrs. Fright," said Doctor Ghastly,
"I'm afraid Scary has come down with a terrifying
case of . . . Human-i-tis."

"Eeeh-eeeh-ahh-ahh!" Mama screamed.

Papa just fainted.

"We must work fast," the doctor said. "Or soon, Scary might start playing in the sun and drinking chocolate milk. Worst of all, she may EVEN like stories with . . . happy endings!"

Papa fainted again.

Quickly, the doctor mixed together a medicine for Scary.

"First, I pour the bubbling brew of a bug into
a mug," she explained. "Then, a sprinkle of
witches' warts. Finally, I add thirteen teardrops
from a dragonfly's eyes."

Scary drank the medicine. Everyone waited

to see what would happen.

First, she howled.

"That's more like it," Mama cackled.

Then, she growled.

"It worked!" screamed Papa.

"Can we go home now?" asked Scary. "I want to play with my kitten."

"Oh, lizard's gizzards!" Papa gasped.

"I'm all right, Papa," Scary told him. "I still love being a monster. I just like kittens, butter- flies, and rainbows too!"

"But monsters are supposed to be scary," Papa
insisted.

"I scared you and Mama," Scary said.

"She's right! She did give us quite a fright,"
Mama added.

Papa thought for a moment. "Let's go home,"
he said with a toothy smile.

HOME AGAIN

By the time they got home, the sun was just
starting to rise. Grandma Gloom howled good-
bye and flew off.

Scary and Baby Boo put on their pajamas.
Then they washed their claws, brushed their
fangs, and crawled into bed.

Papa read them a terrifying bedtime story.
Mama came and tucked them in.

"No matter what you do," Mama told Scary,
"we still think you are a terrible monster."

"And I think you and Papa and Baby Boo are
terrible too," Scary snarled.

"Rotten dreams," Mama said. She gave them
each a big, slimy kiss.

"Sweet nightmares," Papa growled. Then he kissed them, and turned out the light. And all was quiet until . . .

"Thhhhh . . . ank you," shrieked Baby Boo.

"Oh, NO!" Mama screamed.

"Here we go again!" Papa yowled.

Scary just smiled,

and drifted horribly off to sleep.